What are we going to
do now, Frankie?

I don't know, Sal.

I think we've done it all. We've played every sport ever invented,

painted more pictures in a day than van Gogh did in a lifetime,

baked enough cookies to feed a small country,

played every board game we could find,

read every comic book th—

OK, OK. Let's stop talking for ten seconds.

All right. Ten seconds of nothing.

That's it!

Let's Do Nothing!

Tony Fucile

CANDLEWICK PRESS

We can pretend we're a couple of those statues you see in the park. You know, the ones carved out of stone and stuff.

Frankie, what are you doing?

Shooing pigeons is NOT doing nothing. Let's try it again, OK?
Uh… let's imagine we're in a quiet grove in the middle of an old forest.
We'll be two giant redwood trees. You can do that.

I can do that.

Frankie?

YOUR DOG JUST WENT
TO THE BATHROOM ON ME!

You mean that dog, over there?
The one sleeping on my bed?

You know the Empire State Building in New York? You are it.
Tall. Heavy. You've been sitting still for years and years.
No silly pigeon or puny dog could rattle the likes of you,
O Majestic One. Can you DO it, sir?

YEAH!

How's it goin' up there, my friend?

OK, OK. New plan. I'm going to make you the King of the Nothing Doers. Lie down on the floor, please.

Like this?

YES. Now don't move. And you've got to hold your breath. That one on your belly is moving up and down.

Got it.
What if I need to blink?

Mmmmm…

This is BIG.
This is REALLY BIG.
You know what we have to do now,
don'tcha?

Yep.

LET'S
DO
SOMETHING!

To Sal and Frankie (the originals),
Stacey, Eli, and Elinor

First paperback edition 2012

Library of Congress Cataloging-in-Publication Data is available.

Library of Congress Catalog Card Number 2008935654

ISBN 978-0-7636-5269-2 (paperback)

16 17 APS 10 9 8 7 6 5 4

Printed in Humen, Dongguan, China

This book was typeset in Myriad Tilt.
The illustrations were done in ink, colored pencil, and acrylic on watercolor paper.

Candlewick Press
99 Dover Street
Somerville, Massachusetts 02144

visit us at www.candlewick.com